ZHEJIANGOPTERUS

DRYPTOSAURUS

YANGCHUANOSAURUS

AMAZONSAURUS

KILESKUS

ANGATURAMA

GASTONIA

BRACHYCERATOPS

TAPUIASAURUS

# JANE YOLEN

## How Do Dinosaurs Learn to

## READ?

### Illustrated by

# MARK TEAGUE

THE BLUE SKY PRESS

An Imprint of Scholastic Inc. · New York

THE BLUE SKY PRESS

*Celebrating 25 Years of Award-winning Publishing*

Text copyright © 2018 by Jane Yolen
Illustrations copyright © 2018 by Mark Teague

Library of Congress catalog card number: 2017028717

ISBN 978-1-338-23301-8

10 9 8 7 6 5 4 3 2 1     18 19 20 21 22

Printed in Malaysia        108
First edition, July 2018

Book design by Kathleen Westray

For my mother, who taught me to read.

Because I never got to thank her.

—J. Y.


To Kathy Westray, with gratitude.

—M. T.

How does a dinosaur

learn how to read?

Does he skim through the pages

with powerful speed?

Does he use his new book

as a shovel or bat?

Play fetch with the dog?

Throw books

at the cat?

Does he sound out the words?

Or just take a quick look?

Does she lose her huge temper,

then jump on the book?

Does she flip every page
but not really look through it?
Does she skip the hard words?

Does

a dinosaur

CHEW IT?

ANGATURAMA

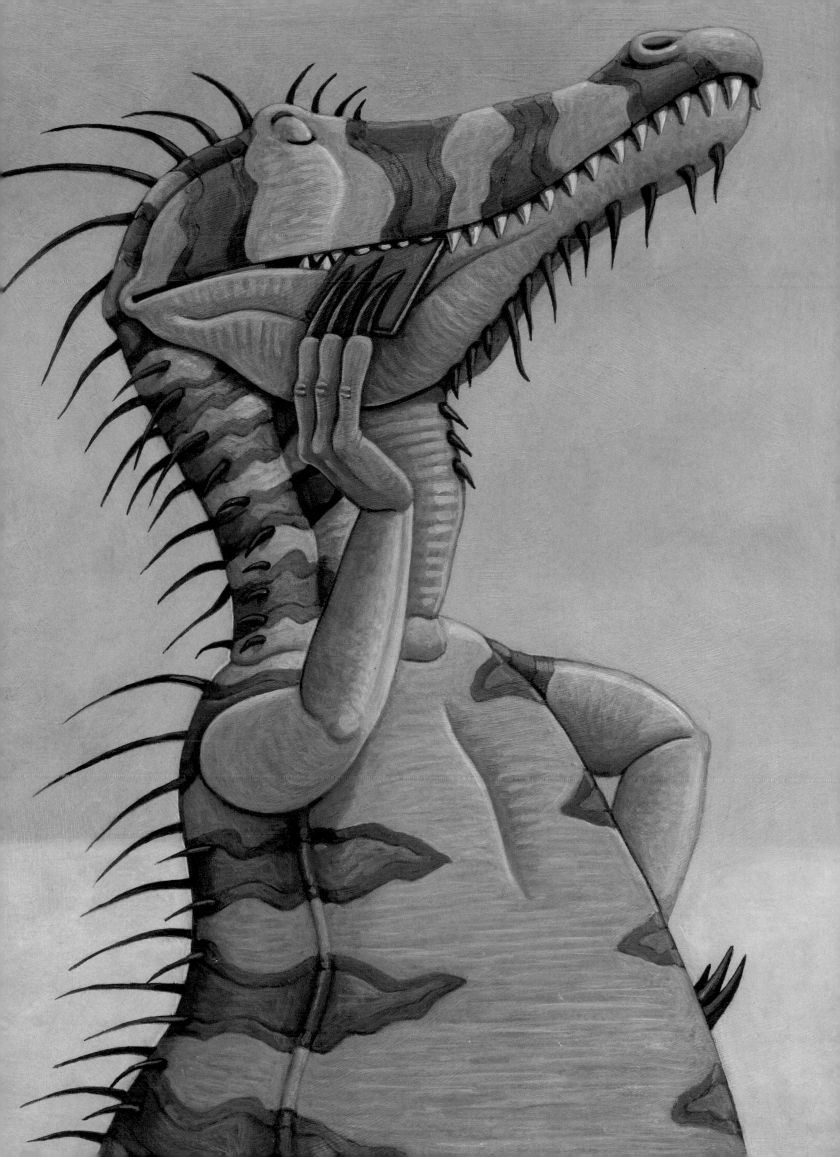

Does he read in the tub,
make the book a big boat,
and then throw a tantrum
when it doesn't float?

Does he read on the potty,

while making a mess?

Does he stay till the end

of the book?

Well—

I guess!

Does she scratch off the words

with the tip of her tail?

Does he have a big hissy
when reading skills fail?

Does a dinosaur

WAIL?

No—she's kind to each book,
to the cover and pages.
She reads very carefully.
Never has rages.

ZHEJIANGOPTERUS

She reads out each word,
till she knows they sound right.
When she snuggles in bed,
Mama turns down the light.

Then he calls to his parents,
who stand by the door,
"Please, Mama, please, Papa,
can I read one more?"

"Tomorrow, tomorrow,
little dinosaur."

For more about how dinosaurs
learn to read, turn the page!

## ABOUT READING

There are many ways to learn to read.

It's a *huge* help when Mama and Papa—and others—
read books aloud to little dinosaurs. The more the better!

Reading aloud helps little dinosaurs in lots and lots of ways—
and they begin to identify sounds, learn words, and enjoy books!

Sometimes they remember the words—or some of them—and
chant along. Sometimes after a book is read aloud, little dinosaurs
who remember the words can match them to the pictures.

Rhyming words can help them remember. And fun, engaging
pictures can bring them back to a favorite book again
and again. *All* of the books in this dinosaur series are
written with rhyming words.

Soon little dinosaurs learn every letter of the alphabet.

Aa  Bb  Cc  Dd  Ee  Ff  Gg  Hh  Ii

Jj  Kk  Ll  Mm  Nn  Oo  Pp  Qq  Rr

Ss  Tt  Uu  Vv  Ww  Xx  Yy  Zz

When a dinosaur knows
letter sounds, it's easier to learn
simple words.

If you sound out every letter,
reading skills will get much better!

Some words in this book begin with the letter sounds below. Let's use them as examples. Mama, Papa, and others help little dinosaurs learn them. Try it! Can *you* say the words?

Dd → dog
This dinosaur and his dog run,
after reading time is done.

Cc → cat
This dinosaur pets her cat.
Then they have a lovely chat.

Bb → bed
This dinosaur reads in bed,
stories filling up his head.

Jj → jump
This dinosaur can jump and yell.
I jump and yell and learn to spell.

Now little dinosaurs use dog, cat, bed, and jump in one sentence:

This dog and cat
jump on the bed.
This dinosaur reads
a book instead!

Can you find the words dog, cat, bed, and jump in this book?
What other words can you read?

Here are more letters and sounds:

Tt → tub
This dinosaur plays in the tub.
He gives ducky a great big scrub.

Mm → Mama
This dinosaur goes for a ride,
she and Mama side by side.

Rr → read
This dinosaur loves to read.
She goes through books with great speed.

Can you find the words tub, Mama, and read in this book?

Here's a big word you see a lot in this book:

# dinosaur

Can you say it?

Can you roar like a big dinosaur?

Can you find the word
dinosaur in this book?

Read to friends.
They'll read to you.
That's what
dinosaurs can do!

ZHEJIANGOPTERUS

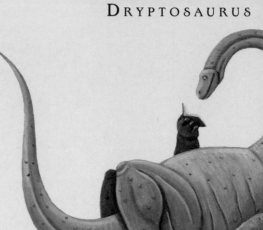

DRYPTOSAURUS

YANGCHUANOSAURUS

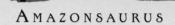

AMAZONSAURUS

KILESKUS

ANGATURAMA

GASTONIA

BRACHYCERATOPS

TAPUIASAURUS

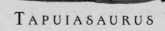